T0413594

WATERFOWL HUNTING

BY CHRISTOPHER FOREST

childsworld.com

Published by The Child's World®
800-599-READ • www.childsworld.com

Photography Credits
Photographs ©: Brian A Smith/Shutterstock Images, cover,
1; Pavel Rodimov/iStockphoto, 5; iStockphoto, 7; Cao
Chunhai/iStockphoto, 9; Red Line Editorial, 10; Steve
Oehlenschlager/Shutterstock Images, 11, 14; Shutterstock
Images, 13, 19; Marc Dufresne/iStockphoto, 17; Suzi
Nelson/Shutterstock Images, 18; Steve Oehlenschlager/
iStockphoto, 21

ISBN Information
9781503869721 (Reinforced Library Binding)
9781503881075 (Portable Document Format)
9781503882386 (Online Multi-user eBook)
9781503883697 (Electronic Publication)

LCCN 2022951233

Printed in the United States of America

ABOUT THE AUTHOR

Christopher Forest is a middle
school teacher in Massachusetts.
He enjoys writing books
for all ages. He has written
nonfiction and fiction stories,
articles, and novels for adults
and children. In his spare time,
he enjoys watching sports,
playing guitar, reading, and
spending time outdoors.

CONTENTS

CHAPTER ONE

POND VISITORS

It was a cool October afternoon at Jordan Pond. Tia and her father waited in their blind, a small portable shelter they set up at the pond's edge. They watched the sky, looking for birds flying south. It was Tia's first time hunting ducks. She and her father planned to use the ducks they caught in a new recipe.

Soon, Tia heard quacking. A flock of ducks emerged from behind a cloud. Some of the birds dove down and landed in the pond. They began paddling across the water toward Tia and her father. The hunters remained hidden by the shelter. Tia aimed her shotgun at a duck that was about to land. She got the duck's feet in her sights. That's what her father taught her to do when hunting a duck that is descending to land. Before shooting, Tia made sure to check her surroundings. She didn't want to accidentally hit any nearby hunters or animals. Then Tia pulled the trigger on her gun.

Some waterfowl hunters use grasses, reeds, or branches to build blinds.

TYPES OF DUCKS

Ducks are the most popular waterfowl game in North America. There are 32 kinds, or species, of ducks that can be hunted on the continent. These species are divided into three types. Puddle ducks are found on most bodies of water, except oceans. Diving ducks stay near large bodies of water, such as lakes, rivers, and oceans. Sea ducks live near coasts and sometimes the Great Lakes.

The bullet hit the duck. The bird fell into the water with a splash. Tia and her father high-fived. She had successfully hunted her first duck.

Like Tia and her father, many hunters enjoy hunting ducks and other waterfowl. Waterfowl are birds that often live in or near water. They are frequently hunted as **game**. In the United States, people hunt a variety of waterfowl. The most common are ducks, such as mallards and redheads. Waterfowl hunters also hunt geese, including Canada geese and white geese. Others hunt swans and coots. Coots look like ducks but have legs, feet, and beaks like a chicken. Hunting waterfowl takes time, but with practice and a willingness to learn, anyone can become a skilled hunter.

Mallards are a popular target for waterfowl hunters. These ducks can be challenging to hunt. Many people consider them to be one of the best-tasting ducks to eat.

CHAPTER TWO

Why People Hunt Waterfowl

People have hunted waterfowl for thousands of years. Many Native American nations, including the Cree and Chippewa, have traditionally hunted waterfowl for centuries. Some tribes hunted waterfowl for food. Members of some nations also collected feathers to decorate clothing. Others gathered down. Down is the soft layer of feathers close to a waterfowl's skin. It is used as stuffing for pillows and warm clothing.

In the 1600s, people in Europe began using guns to hunt waterfowl. When Europeans settled in North America, they found many types of waterfowl along the coast. Ducks and geese were easy to hunt. They became popular foods in colonial North America. In the 1700s, improvements to guns made it easier for people to hunt waterfowl. By the 1800s, people began selling the waterfowl they hunted for money. The demand for waterfowl grew as more people moved to the United States.

Goose and duck down is soft and fluffy. Clusters of down are commonly used as stuffing in winter coats, bedding, and blankets.

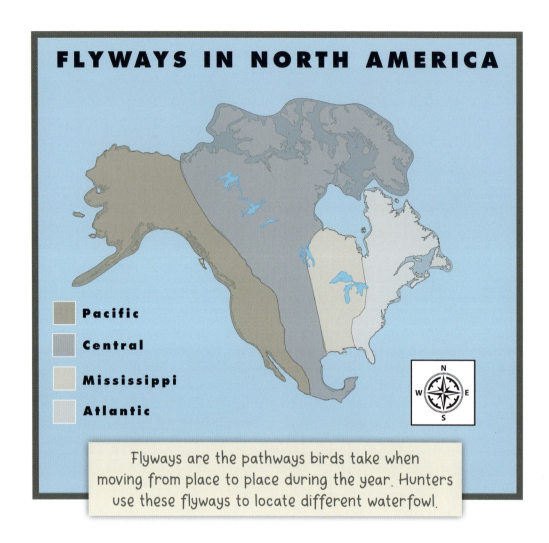

FLYWAYS IN NORTH AMERICA

- Pacific
- Central
- Mississippi
- Atlantic

Flyways are the pathways birds take when moving from place to place during the year. Hunters use these flyways to locate different waterfowl.

By the 1900s, many waterfowl species had been overhunted. Their populations dropped. Leaders in the United States and Canada passed laws to protect the birds. **Conservation** groups purchased land and made it into conservation areas. This helped protect waterfowl **habitats**. Because of these efforts, waterfowl populations rose.

Some waterfowl game hunters use trained hunting dogs. When the hunter shoots a bird, the dog helps locate and retrieve it.

Modern hunters continue to hunt waterfowl. Many enjoy the birds as food. Some hunt waterfowl to keep the populations steady. If the population of ducks and geese gets too large, it can cause problems. The birds might fight for food. Some birds might not have enough to eat. This could make populations drop. For other hunters, waterfowl hunting is a fun sport. This is sometimes called **game hunting**. After shooting waterfowl, hunters might have the birds stuffed. They display the birds as trophies in their homes.

CHAPTER THREE

HUNTING TOOLS AND RULES

Waterfowl hunters can use several different tools. Many use shotguns, which fire bullets called shells. Shells are filled with **shot**. Some hunters prefer using a bow and arrow. The most common type of bow is a compound bow. Compound bows make it easier for hunters to pull back and release the **bowstring** used to fire an arrow.

Some hunters use special devices to make hunting easier. Many use decoys, or realistic models of waterfowl. Decoys float in water. They lure waterfowl to a body of water by making it seem safe. The waterfowl think the decoys are real birds and land near them, where hunters are waiting. Other hunters use a call to lure waterfowl to them. Calls often sound like a cross between a whistle and a wooden flute. They mimic the sounds of waterfowl.

Some people hunt from blinds. Waterfowl hunters often set up blinds near the water to help them stay hidden from birds.

A hunter should always treat her shotgun
as if it is loaded. She should make sure
her gun is pointed only at the target.

In some states, hunters must leave the wings or heads of waterfowl intact so the birds can be properly identified. This way, state agencies can keep track of waterfowl populations.

They wait in a blind until birds come near. Elevated blinds are raised off the ground. Blinds set up on the ground are called ground blinds. Many ground blinds can be moved from place to place. This way, people can hunt in different locations.

A hunter should also be aware of hunting rules in her state. Some states set limits on the number of birds that can be hunted.

These are called bag limits. Bag limits help keep bird populations balanced and stable. Without limits, waterfowl species might be overhunted. A hunter should have a hunting license, too. This gives a hunter permission to hunt. People can usually purchase hunting licenses from outdoor sports stores. In the United States, duck hunters must also have a Federal Duck Stamp. This gives hunters permission from the government to hunt ducks.

Waterfowl hunters should also know when waterfowl hunting season begins and ends. Hunting season is the only time of year hunters can legally hunt waterfowl. Usually, waterfowl hunting season is in fall or winter. By this time of year, female waterfowl have already laid eggs and raised their young. This means that baby birds are able to survive on their own. Many waterfowl also **migrate** during fall and winter, resting in bodies of water along the way.

MIGRATORY BIRD TREATY ACT

Hunters must be aware of **federal regulations** that protect waterfowl. The Migratory Bird Treaty Act protects 1,100 species of migrating birds in the United States, including waterfowl. One rule says birds cannot be baited. This means hunters cannot use food, salt, or grain to lure waterfowl. There are also rules about hunting over crop fields, which attract many birds. People can hunt over flooded crops or fields where seeds have been scattered by normal agricultural practices, such as harvesting. But people cannot hunt near fields where grain is stored or where seeds have been scattered by mowing, trampling, or chemical treatments. This is because the scattered seeds in these areas could act as bait.

CHAPTER FOUR

CONSERVATION AND SAFETY

Waterfowl hunters should follow several safety guidelines. Hunters should always be aware of their surroundings. They should know where they are, where they're going, and where other hunters are. This helps hunters avoid injuring themselves or others. It helps them avoid getting lost, too. Hunters should also know how to use hunting tools such as shotguns safely. They should never randomly fire in the air or at the water while hunting. This could result in the accidental shooting of other animals or hunters.

It's important for hunters to be prepared, too. Hunters should always carry their hunting license and any stamps required by their state and country. They should also wear the proper hunting gear. This may include waders, a type of plastic or rubber pants that cover a hunter's clothes. Waders allow hunters to enter the water without getting their clothes wet. If hunting from a boat, hunters should wear life jackets. Other people wear bright orange vests or hats to make them stand out to other hunters.

Beginners can take hunter education classes to practice handling weapons such as bows. They learn to aim accurately and use their weapons safely.

Wearing waders helps waterfowl hunters stay warm and dry in cold wetlands, lakes, rivers, and marshes.

This prevents accidental shootings. Hunters should also carry cell phones in case of emergencies. They can keep their phones in waterproof plastic bags.

It's important for hunters to be conservation-minded, too. This means that they care about wildlife and the environment. They treat waterfowl and their habitats respectfully while outdoors.

If hunting from a boat, people should travel in a group, be prepared for emergencies, and avoid going out on the water in bad weather.

BANDED BIRDS

Sometimes hunters might shoot a **banded** bird. These are birds that have a band, or circular piece of metal, attached to their legs. Bands are placed on birds by the Bird Banding Laboratory, an organization run by the US Geological Survey. It has been banding birds since 1920. The bands help identify birds. They also track where birds migrate and how long they live. Hunters can shoot banded birds. But they should report the birds they shoot to the lab. This helps the lab keep track of bird data. The lab has banded more than 77 million birds.

Hunters should always follow rules about the size and number of waterfowl they can hunt. They should never hunt birds outside of the hunting season.

Conservation-minded hunters should also avoid leaving litter or leftover shot behind. Otherwise, animals might accidentally eat the litter, which could cause them to become sick or die. Hunters should be particularly careful with bullets. These often contain materials such as lead, which can be deadly to animals.

Some hunters join conservation groups. These groups help care for wetlands and waterfowl habitats. They teach others how to hunt waterfowl responsibly. There are hunter education classes for beginners, too. These classes help beginners learn how to hunt safely. By following the rules and making responsible choices, hunters can keep the tradition of waterfowl hunting alive.

Experienced hunters can help protect waterfowl by teaching beginners to make responsible choices and respect wildlife.

GLOSSARY

banded (BAN-ded) A banded bird has a circular piece of metal placed around its leg. Banded birds help researchers keep track of birds' ages and migration habits.

bowstring (BOH-string) A bowstring is the string on a bow. A hunter pulls on the bowstring and releases it to shoot an arrow.

conservation (kon-sur-VAY-shuhn) Conservation is the protection of wildlife and other natural resources. Conservation groups protect waterfowl habitats.

federal regulations (FED-ur-uhl reg-yuh-LAY-shuhns) Federal regulations are rules created by a country's government. There are some federal regulations hunters need to follow in order to protect wildlife populations.

game (GAME) Animals hunted for sport are called game. Ducks are the most popular type of waterfowl game in North America.

game hunting (GAME HUNT-ing) Game hunting is the act of hunting animals for sport or fun. People who enjoy game hunting sometimes shoot ducks or other waterfowl.

habitats (HAB-i-tatz) Habitats are places where animals live. Conservation groups work to protect waterfowl habitats.

migrate (MY-grayt) To migrate is to travel from one area or region to another. Many waterfowl migrate during fall and winter.

shot (SHOT) Shot is a type of small pellet put into a shell that is used as a bullet. Hunters should be careful not to spill shot when waterfowl hunting.

FAST FACTS

- Waterfowl are birds that spend time on bodies of water. Ducks, geese, swans, and coots are all types of waterfowl.

- People have hunted waterfowl for thousands of years. Some people eat waterfowl for food. Others use waterfowl down for blankets, coats, and pillows.

- In the 1900s, the US government passed laws to help the waterfowl population grow. One law is called the Migratory Bird Treaty Act.

- Many hunters use shotguns or bows and arrows to hunt waterfowl.

- Some people use decoys or calls to help lure waterfowl. Others hunt from blinds to stay hidden from waterfowl.

- It is important for hunters to shoot only the waterfowl they need in order to keep the bird population stable.

ONE STRIDE FURTHER

- Some hunters use calls to lure waterfowl. Others use decoys. Compare and contrast these hunting methods. If you were waterfowl hunting, which method would you use and why?

- How does hunting waterfowl help keep animal populations balanced?

- How is waterfowl hunting with a bow and arrow similar to hunting waterfowl with a shotgun? How is it different? Which tool would you rather use for hunting?

FIND OUT MORE

IN THE LIBRARY

Bell, Samantha S. *Firearm Safety*. Parker, CO: The Child's World, 2024.

Kingston, Seth. *Hunting*. New York, NY: PowerKids Press, 2022.

Uhl, Xina M., and Philip Wolny. *Insider Tips for Hunting Waterfowl*. New York, NY: Rosen Central, 2018.

ON THE WEB

Visit our website for links about waterfowl hunting:

childsworld.com/links

Note to Parents, Caregivers, Teachers, and Librarians: We routinely verify our Web links to make sure they are safe and active sites. So encourage your readers to check them out!

INDEX